All the Characters have no exis
of the Author, and have no relation w
name or

The are not even distantly inspired o
to the Author and all in

GW00871160

The Orphanage

John Finan

authorHOUSE®

AuthorHouse™ UK Ltd.
500 Avebury Boulevard
Central Milton Keynes, MK9 2BE
www.authorhouse.co.uk
Phone: 08001974150

First published by AuthorHouse 9/26/2011

ISBN: 978-1-4567-8018-0 (sc)
ISBN: 978-1-4567-8019-7 (e)

The Beginning

Michael looks around the restaurant noticing all the people. It's as if they had not eaten for weeks. Big mouths, small mouths, chewing, drinking. He smiles to himself and thinks the toilets will be busy with this crowd later on. The waiter approaches him and he asks for coffee and toast. His stomach is not so good and his head is sore, too much alcohol last night. 'I will have to give it up' he thinks, 'those late nights with the boys. It takes it's toll, only for that vodka I drank last night', he thinks, 'I might be eating something more solid this morning.' The doctor warned him to cut back or cut it out but with these nightmares he was having lately it was either drink or pills to help him sleep. It's a while since he was back in Galway. It must be ten years since himself and the boys played here in Salthill. Still last night was busy. Some of the fans are a bit old but it was still nice to see them again.

They played a different song last night, by request, and it had them all clapping and singing. "The Boys are back in Town" was the name of the song. They played it at their last concert as well.

Michael holds a cup to his mouth with his two hands conscious that people are looking at him. The coffee is warm and he feels himself coming around with the second drink. The toast will have to wait he thinks.

He sees the waiter staring at him as if he knows what he is thinking. He beckons him forward and asks him for more coffee.

"Would you like anything else?" The waiter asks a slight grin on his face.

"No," Michael replies, "and keep your coffee, I am going for a walk" he says getting up from his table.

"I am sorry, Sir" the waiter says.

"So am I" Michael replies walking through the reception. At the reception desk Michael asks that man at the counter to take a message. "Tell Jim and Tom in room 31 and Dennis in room 32 that I am going for a walk and that I will see them this evening at 7 o'clock".

The receptionist smiles back at Michael saying "No problem Sir, I am here all day."

"Thanks." Michael says as he walks out the main door. The receptionist looks at him walking away. His jeans and leather jacket smell of stale beer and thinks 'only for your money, lad you would not be stopping here or your friends with you. People like you give this place a bad name,' and he goes back to answering the phone.

It starts to rain a small bit as Michael walks down the concrete steps. Looking up and down he lights a cigarette. He walks down to the left of the building, crossing the road he looks into the record store. He leaves very quickly 'not able for that noise' he thinks, 'not yet anyway.' He sees an off licence on the corner, walking into it he asks for a brandy. The lady smiles at him saying it is a nice day. Michael does not notice her and just puts the change in his pocket and walks out again. Walking around the back of the building, he notices some cats at the bends and an old man sitting in the corner crying. Going over to him Michael asks "What is wrong with you?"

The old man replies "I am short a bit of money. I slept here last night, but when I woke up my money was gone."

"Here," Michael says, "take this, it will help you, it will give you a 'bit of a buzz.' Keep it," Michael says, "I will get another." as he walks down the small alley way.

The old man smiles, looking after him saying "Thank you son, thank you".

As he takes the corner and looks around he notices that the traffic has stopped and that people are staring up the lane at something. 'What?' He wonders. Walking up towards the path he notices a funeral coming down and turning right towards the funeral home. Moving towards the wall behind him he stares at the hearse and blesses himself. As the crowd slowly moves away he turns around and stares at the building in front of him. He didn't want to come here, it was by accident he arrived here but it was as fate decided. He was standing outside his old home. The place he was reared in and hated. The building two hundred yards in front of him was his home or prison for years, the orphanage. He slowly opens the small gate and walks up the laneway. It's closed now for the last number of years. The windows are broken but the structure stands out as the deadly nightmare it was. Sitting down on a large stone outside he lights a cigarette. 'If I had a drink of brandy it would help too,' he thinks. Blowing the smoke out in front of him, he thinks of the first day he came here. A day like today, wet, miserable and his only good memory was his father smiling as he said goodbye.

Chapter 1

"Goodbye Michael. I will be home at Christmas – please God. You will be alright here for a while." Michael waves goodbye to his father, he never did come back. He heard later that he died in England at the spuds. He was never the same man since his wife died. Wiping the tears from his eyes Michael is led towards a large building by a priest, Father Johnson. His father and the priest had met before at his mother's funeral. His face like a stone, cold and pale.

Michael was to learn later that this man was not to be trusted. He had a bad temper which caused him a horrible death in later years. "This is your home now young man, make the best of it. You will sleep in a single room tonight; tomorrow you will sign in for school and sleep in the large dormitory with the rest of the boys". As the priest opens the door of the room Michael puts his bag on the ground. Looking out the small window he notices it snowing. Sitting on the bed Michael takes out a medal from his pocket which was given to him by his mother. Crying, he looks at it and says to himself, "Look after me

Mammy I am on my own and need your help." Lying down on the bed with his clothes on, he looks up at the ceiling. Closing his eyes he dreams of years ago as a small child, his father coming from the bog and his mother standing at the door, her face lit up with excitement.

Her last words to Michael on her death bed were "Don't worry love I will always be with you, you will never be alone". Holding the medal she gave him, Michael opened his eyes to the still sound of the large building. He covered himself with a rough sheet, putting the medal in his pocket he goes to sleep.

Chapter 2

Michael awakens to the noise outside the window. Climbing outside the bed he notices he slept with his trousers on last night. Looking out the window he sees a large crowd of young people standing outside the front gates. Lined up in two rows like an army. Rubbing his eyes he runs down the hallway towards the stairs. Meeting a priest he asks "What is going on outside?" He gets no answer only a sign to move on. As he moves down the stairs outside he notices that a crowd of boys are standing in a straight line, about twenty of them moving towards the entrance. He pulls his trousers up and joins them. One of the priests watching him shouts "Come over here young man, what is your name?" he asks.

"Michael O'Brien."

"Michael O'Brien what?" the priests asks with a stern voice.

"Michael O'Brien, what is yours?"

The priest raises his hand and gives him a slap in the face. "While you are here, you will address me as `Father', understand?"

Michael rubs his face and walks towards the other boys. Looking back at the priest he thinks, 'you ugly sow with a big belly.' Michael walks over towards the boys who were lined up just inside the gate. Looking either side of him he notices two black boys and a Chinese boy. Rubbing his eyes Michael looks at the priest approaching him. "I am Father James" he says, "I am principal of this establishment, this is my vice-principal Father Michael, you will obey the rules here or you will be punished. There is school time and sports time. You are not allowed to leave this school, only with a priest or guardian. You will work two days a week in the fields, sowing and digging potatoes, carrots etc. The vegetables will be cleaned by you on your turns. Collect your clothing from your rooms and gather together in the main hall."

Walking back towards the building Michael looks at the fields at the back and thinks 'some donkey work', he knew about it at home with his father. Putting his clothes in a bag he moved towards the main hall. He hears a voice from behind him. Looking behind him he sees a small boy limping. "What happened to you?" he asked.

"I had an accident playing football. I am here a month, you are new here?" he says.

"Yes." Michael replied, "I came in here yesterday."

"My name is John Dempsey what is yours?" the boy asked.

"Michael" he replies. "What is it like in here?" Michael asked the young lad.

"Rough," the boy replied, "watch your back. Some of the priests are alright, helpful enough. Some of them would cane you for the least thing."

Michael looks around the hall, the light shining through the window. The big holy picture staring down at him in a ghostly fashion. He notices the priest walking in the main door. Standing up under the cross he opened up a small book. "I will read your names out and your number and your duties for the next week." When Michael's name is read out he is told the number of his bed. Going back to his room he collects a small case and moves towards the large room. There are about forty beds in two lines. The lad he met in the hallway smiles up at him from a few beds down. The stillness of the room is disturbed by the sound of a loud voice. "My name is Father Johnson." the priest says. "You will obey my orders while you are in this establishment or you will pay the price with this." he says, holding a cane in his hand. "As and from today you will make your beds every morning before you go to breakfast and you will attend church before you go to your classrooms."

Michael looks up at him with a vengeful eye. 'You are one thick looking so and so, that big mouth of yours is too big for your face.' he thinks.

The priest also shouts, "You will spend two days a week in the fields digging spuds, working and cleaning the gardens."

Slowly, as the room fills up, everyone goes to their beds. There are some lonesome faces, either they have no parents or they have been taken away from them for different reasons. Michael goes back to his book. He notices a lot of children looking at the shadow of the door. It's the shadow of a priest, Father Johnson. Looking around Michael notices him grinning at some of the boys. 'You come near me, I will leave a few scares on your face' he thinks. As the bell rings the other priest motions the children to the classrooms. As the children move in and sit down Michael sees some older girls mopping and cleaning in the main hall. They have very short hair, all with sad faces. Michael talks to the boy beside him and asks. "When do we eat?"

"We will be told that shortly." the boy replies.

Another priest enters the room and writes on the board starting with Monday to Friday, what time meals are at, what time classes begin etc. His name is Father Laverty. Himself and Michael will become good friends. "Now it is time to eat you can move towards the lunch room upstairs and we will have breakfast." As the boys move out of the classroom, Michael looks out the window towards the garden. The sun is shining after the snow. He watches a young man cleaning the leaves off the ground. Looking at the man through the glass he notices he is wearing a ring on his ear and he is humming a song. The window is half open and Michael thinks the song is a welcome boost to such a depressed atmosphere. Moving towards the kitchen he notices the steam coming out the door. As he sits down at the table three boys sit beside him. "Hello lads, what's your names?" he asks.

The boys shake hands with him not saying a word. The one in front of him smiles and hums a tune. Michael smiles back at him and thinking 'that's the tune the man in the garden was humming a few minutes ago.'

Chapter 3

Nothing much changed in the next six months. Michael got used to the place, worked in the fields two days a week. Hard work digging potatoes and weeding gardens. The other three days in school, learning Irish, maths and history. Sometimes, when he was alone in the fields, he cried. Looking up at the mountains he thought about home. His mother working outside feeding the hens and ducks. Michael standing beside her, his face all red and her singing away to herself. Every night before bed he would look at the medal she gave him and ask her to watch over him. Michael made very few friends in the place. The priests were no ways friendly. They gave you work to do and you did it or you got caned. Discipline was very strict. Father Johnson was the worst; if you crossed him the beating he would give you would bring a smile to his face. It happened one morning when Michael woke up. He was shouting at a lad named Jim. Michael ate with him a few mornings at breakfast. As the priest lifted his hand to hit him Michael shouted "Leave him alone."

Father Johnson was shouting "Hand me that instrument."

"I won't" Jim replies, "I found it, and I will keep it."

"Leave him alone." Michael shouts.

The priest walks over to him and slaps him across the face. Michael feels the blood coming from his mouth as he falls on the floor. The priest is about to lift the cane again when a loud voice shouts behind him.

"Leave those boys alone." It's the caretaker from outside. Hearing the shouting he ran in a panic.

The priest looks back at him; his eyes mad with temper and says "Mind your own business."

"You touch those lads again," he replies, "You will be eating hospital food for a long time".

The priest throws the cane on the ground and walks out talking to himself. The caretaker lifts Michael on to the bed and rubs a hanky around his mouth.

"Take it easy lads." he says. "It is not the first run in I had with that cowboy."

Rubbing his face Michael says "Thanks, it is nice to know somebody cares."

It was later Michael discovered who the man was; he was a caretaker in the place. He was always a help to the boys.

Michael goes over to Jim in the bed and says "Are you alright?"

"Not too bad," he replies, "except for this", showing Michael his back with the tracks on it.

"What did he want?" Michael asked.

"This." Jim replied holding it out in front of him.

"A mouth organ." Michael replies.

"Yes." says Jim, "You keep it for a while. That cowboy could come back at any time."

"Thanks." Michael says blowing into it; "I will take care of it. And thank you Sir." he shouts down to the caretaker on the lawn as he puts the instrument in his pocket.

Michael discovered after some time that it was the caretaker who gave it to Jim after he found it in a bin outside the building. That night Michael put it under his pillow with his mother's locket before going to sleep. 'I will give it to Jim next week,' he thinks, 'when we are in the field picking spuds.'

Chapter 4

As the year rolled on and the autumn weather set in, Michael spent a lot of time indoors. There was no television, just some 'Beano' and 'Dandy' comics which some of the older boys picked up from the paper man. Every night, Michael was given the arduous task of washing the kitchen floor. Afterwards, he would take some milk from the fridge and the next day leave some out for the cats and a few breadcrumbs on the windowsill for the birds. Looking at the birds through the window, the singing would bring a smile to his face in the morning. Some days, when he was working in the fields, he noticed how they stayed close to him in the nearby trees. Some nights, when lying in the bed, a small field mouse would show his face at the corner of the room. Michael would slowly move his hand into his pocket and leave some cheese beside him. Smiling he would think, 'He has no family, a field mouse coming into an orphanage.' During the school classes, Michael would look out the window and sometimes he would see one the birds he was feeding looking in at him, the goldfinch. His father used to catch them and put them in a cage at the fireplace. The chirping would bring a smile to anybody's face.

Father Lafferty was their history teacher. Michael liked him; he would talk to him about the druids and the Irish famine. Michael liked reading the history book especially about Ireland. He liked it when Father Lafferty would speak to him about nature, 'the birds and the bees' and how they survived in the harsh world outside against man and other animals. The choir singing was also something he liked. He did not sing himself but sometimes, outside the church, himself and some of the boys would hum a tune or two they heard from somewhere. It was during the choir practice that he met a lad named Tom. Michael asked him his last name but he would not give it. The two of them would sit outside the church talking about music. Tom told him his mother played the piano before she died. He lived with his uncle for a while himself and his sister. They lived with another relation for a while but the law decided that they would be better off in an orphanage. Tom and his sister were separated by the Courts and the two were sent to different places. They tried to hold on to her but the day came they took her away. He swore if the ever got his freedom he would find her. He did find her in later years, in Galway. She had got married and had two kids, two boys. They always kept in contact after that. Tom told him things about his family that shocked Michael. His mother was very sick. Tom had to look after her up till the time she died. No help from anybody. His father was a waster and many a beating he gave him. Michael could see the hatred in his eyes when he talked. Michael and Tom became good friends. They would talk for hours at the back of the church about music. Tom had a love for music. He often laid in bed at night time when he was younger; his mother played the piano and sung him to sleep. Sometimes they would hear music outside coming from a van or car. Tom would hum the music to Michael for a half an hour. Michael would put an extra melody to it with his lilting as Tom would sing. They would meet at the back of the church every week. The priest would look at him very suspiciously, especially when they would start lilting or singing. Michael only played the mouth organ on his own. He borrowed it from Jim every Saturday and gave it back on Monday. Tom never asked him for it and Michael told him it was not his. It was at a later stage that Jim met him and they played together at the back of the church. Jim would blow the mouth organ, Michael and Tom would beat the dustbins with sticks. The music would give them a lift and the three boys would dance to the beat of the blues. No singing, just music. It was at this stage that Jim held on to the mouth organ. He would not give it to anybody, even Michael. When the music finished Jim would put the mouth organ in his pocket, no one, but no one would take it from him.

Chapter 5

Christmas came along. Michael stands at the window looking at the white snow. He sees the robins in the field in front of him. Taking some crumbs from his pocket, he leaves them on the window sill. There are no decorations around the place, just a crib in the church. The only sound around is the priest's footsteps on the tiles. Looking at his mother's medal, he imagines he sees her face shining through the window. Holding his hands together he says "Happy Christmas, Mammy". Putting the medal in his pocket, he dries his eyes and dresses himself. Walking down the stairs, Michael notices a young boy standing in the corner. Looking at him, he sees he is crying. "What is wrong?" he asks. The boy dries his eyes with his hands and shows Michael the photograph. It is the picture of a band. "Who are they?" Michael asked. The boy points to one of them in the picture. "Who is it?" Michael asks.

"My father", the boy replies. The picture shows four people, one playing drums, three playing guitars. "They took me away from him six months ago. He got into trouble with drink and they put me in here."

Michael had noticed him around the place; he was al
on his own. "What's your name?" he asked.

"Dennis" he replies.

"Here take this" Michael says giving him a hanky. "Dry
yourself and let's see what Christmas brings."

The two boys walk up the hall. Michael with his hand
around his shoulder. Sad, but the way they walk up the
main hall with the sun shining in the window, it would be
hard to believe they met only two minutes before.

Chapter 6

After the breakfast Michael and Dennis entered the main building where the Christmas tree was. A tree with lights and a fairy on top shines away above the rest of the crowd. As the boys start to walk down to the presents, two priests walk by them shouting "There will be Mass first then we will see what happens, come on boys it is time to pray."

The large contingent of boys moved slowly out the main door. As Michael moves out he hears the organ and a low voice singing. "God help us" he laughs, "that voice is bad. It is like a barrel ready to burst" he says to Dennis beside him. Father O'Malley is playing the organ. The singer is a priest who came for the Christmas. He arrived a week ago. Looking up at the priest as he entered the church, Michael thinks to himself 'he is not bad but that gobshite singing would give a headache to an elephant.' As Michael moves up the church Dennis and himself sit down in the second seat. As the church filled up Michael notices something very strange. Dennis starts humming some tune. It's not the hymn. The melody of the music he heard him humming in the playground last week on his own. Michael's listening is disturbed by the movement of a priest, Father Johnson. Hitting the boy across the head he shouts "Quiet you thug".

The organ stops playing and Father O'Malley rushes down the stairs shouting "What's wrong with you?" he says to the priest.

As the two priests meet Father O'Malley looks at Dennis crying. "What happened you young fellow?" he asks.

Dennis doesn't answer just points to the other priest "What did you hit the lad for?" he shouts at the priest.

Father Johnson replies, "He was grinning at the music."

"I was not," the boy replied, "I was not".

Father Johnson moved towards the boy again to hit him. Michael stands in front of him blocking his hand. "I will put manners on you too" the priest shouts.

"You will hit nobody." Father O'Malley shouts standing in front of him. "It is Christmas, leave well enough alone."

Michael hands Dennis the hanky saying "Take it easy."

Father Johnson storms out of the chapel shouting "I wish I had more authority here, maybe someday I will".

"Not if I have my way" the other priest replies. As Father O'Malley walks back to the organ to continue playing he stares down at the lad with the handkerchief and says "Would you like to sing young man?"

Dennis replies "Sing what?"

"Silent Night" the priest says. All eyes are watching him from the church. "They call you Dennis?" the priest says.

"That's my name" the boy replies.

As the priest starts to play the organ, Dennis coughs out a spit and takes a drink of water. The other priest sits down with a frown on his face. All the other boys in the church look up at him and they start singing. His voice is sweet to the sound of the organ. He increases his tone slowly and the organ stops playing. To the whole congregation, it brings a warm feeling of hope and courage. As he stops singing the church goes quiet. Only the trickle of water makes a sound on the window. Climbing down the chairs, Dennis walks back to his seat smiling. He blesses himself in front of Michael saying "Happy Christmas friend".

The Christmas day went alright. A large crowd of boys filled the main hall. Legs of chicken, no turkey, and vegetables were served on the tables. Dessert included 'custard and jelly'. It was after the meal that the fun really started. As the boys moved around the Christmas tree Michael picks up a parcel. Opening it he finds comics, 'Beano' and 'Dandy'. The other boys find various things. A young boy finds a tractor, another a bus. It's only as Michael looks across at Dennis he smiles. He is holding a small instrument, a small guitar. The simple thing and the smile on his face showed Michael that he is happy with what he got. The priests walk beside the young boys each of them with a stern look on his face. Michael sees Father Johnson in the far off distance. 'A hated character,' he thinks, 'if he ever raises his hand to me or any of my friends he will pay a hardy price', closing his fist in anger.

At about seven o'clock the priests clapped their hands shouting "Now boys, get some fresh air and we will do some cleaning up later."

The two priests look at one another and Father Lafferty says "It is Christmas time lads, leave your presents here and go out for some air."

Father Johnson shouts "What about all these dishes?"

"They can wait `till tomorrow" the other priest replies.

"You have these young boys ruined." Johnson shouts.

"It's only for one day," Father Lafferty replies, "they deserve that. Now lads, before you go outside I would like you to listen to some records I have. Move towards the corner of the hall please".

Michael looked up at Dennis with the guitar and thinks, 'Maybe in a few years time, maybe.' He holds Dennis' hand and brings him over to the corner. A timid lad Dennis, shy and very frail. It was only in later life he told Michael the whole story. How his dad played music and the relation that gave him a rough time. He had a photograph of his mother in his pocket as well as one of the band. It was given to him by his mother. Walking up the hall, Michael sees a big box in the corner. Father Lafferty opens it and puts a record on. Turning it up, Michael hears the low voice of Mario Lanzo. Everyone in the place holds their heads down, not too impressed. Seeing the lonesome faces the priest goes to the cupboard. "Maybe this one would suit better" he says, changing the record. Michael notices the name of the sleeve, 'The Searchers.' The guitar starts to play and the drum starts to beat. Michael and Dennis smile at one another. Clapping his hands, Michael brings the crowd alive. Looking over at Jim his face lights up and Tom beside him moves his feet to the music. The music seems to bring a Christmas atmosphere to the place. The only music they hear all year is the choir music or a car passing the building.

The sound is disturbed by the shouting of a boy. "Come on Dennis, give me the guitar."

"No." he replies hitting him across the face with it. The boy is John, a bully who pushes everybody around. Michael makes a run for him as he picks up the guitar. John hits Michael in the face with it and breaks it. Dennis goes hysterical shouting "You big bastard." The two priests interfere, holding the two boys back.

Michael holds Dennis back shouting "Don't worry it can be fixed". Father Lafferty pushes John to one side and Father Johnson holds Dennis and Michael.

He gives Dennis a slap in the face saying "You will clean these dishes tomorrow and scrub the hall, and you will help him." he shouts at Michael. "Now, get your things and go to your rooms".

Picking up the broken guitar Dennis puts the pieces under his arm Michael helping him. "Don't worry Dennis it can be fixed."

Father Johnson stares down at the two boys saying "You will be an old man before you fix that piece of rubbish."

'Maybe not as old as you.' Michael thinks to himself. Dennis holds his head down as he passes the two priests. Michael looks at him and the way he holds the broken guitar. You would swear it was part of his body. The room empties out slowly. Looking at all the broken delph and the food stuck to the floor, Michael thinks, 'it will be a busy day tomorrow cleaning all this shit up.' Closing the door behind him he climbs the stairs to his room, he undresses and goes to bed. He holds his mother's medal in his hand kisses it and puts it under the pillow. Looking at the shadow of the window across the room, he thinks, 'a big day tomorrow, cleaning up the garbage.' Smiling, he hopes Dennis and himself can fix the guitar.

Chapter 7

The next morning, Dennis starts cleaning the food off the floor. Using a putty knife, Michael scrapes the tiles while Dennis holds the refuse bag. Michael puts some of the bread in his pocket to feed the birds. As he stacks the chairs, he notices a bit of timber in the corner. Picking it up, he notices its part of the broken guitar. Handing it to Dennis he sees the caretaker up the hall collecting the rubbish. Holding the bit of timber, Denis says "What am I going to do with this Michael, I cannot fix it?"

"Don't worry," Michael replies, "we will get someone to fix it."

As the caretaker comes in to collect the bags, he sees Dennis holding the piece of timber. "What's wrong?" he asks, "Have you broken something?"

"Yes," Michael replies, "Santa Claus got out of hand last night."

"Show me that," the caretaker says, "it's part of a guitar, a small one at that. Have you the other parts?" he asks.

"They are upstairs." Dennis replies.

"Go up and get them", the caretaker says.

Dennis rushes away and comes back in a few minutes holding the strings and the bits of timber, tears forming in his eyes. "You won't fix this." he says.

The caretaker looks at it saying "You made a right mess of this lad, throw it in the bag", he says to Michael. "You like music?" he says to Dennis.

"Yes", he replies rubbing his eyes.

"What about you?" he shouts at Michael.

"It is all we have in this dump" he replies.

"My sister's son has a small one at home, I will fix it and bring it in next week, is that ok?" he says, giving the hanky to Dennis. "In the mean time, just clean the shit off the floor before the big boys show up. I will leave it under the cupboard next Tuesday. Just make sure you hide it somewhere safe". Carrying the bags, the caretaker moves up the hall singing. Michael smiles, looking at Dennis, thinking 'It's not a bad Christmas after all'. "Come on buck it's time for some grub if there is any left." 'Yes,' Michael thinks, 'this caretaker could be an alright buck.'

Everybody watches as Dennis and Michael cross the room. There is not much food left but the cook hands them two small plates of sausages and eggs. "Easy now, it is Christmas. Next week it will be stale bread and porridge." The two boys look around in silence.

"There is something wrong." Michael says as he looks at his food.

"There was an accident last night." one of the boys whispered in his ear. "One of the priests fell down the stairs."

"Who was it?" Michael says.

"They won't tell us". The boy replies. "The two priests were arguing about something at the top of the stairs last night one of them slipped and fell down. It was an accident."

The boys finished their food and walked into the garden. It's cold with the birds jumping in and out of the hedge. Michael throws a few crumbs on the ground watching the ambulance going out the gate. The priests stand at the main door watching Michael and Dennis walking beside them.

'It must be Father O'Malley.' Michael thinks. "If it was that other cowboy it would be no harm" he says to Dennis.

The day passed fairly quickly. The boys were told that night that the priest had a slight injury and that he would be home in two weeks. Michael was glad, he liked the man; he was a good organ player and a nice man to talk to. As Michael pulled the clothes up on him that night, all he thought about was, 'would the caretaker get the guitar or was he joking'.

The next day several families called to the orphanage. In the beginning Michael thought they were relatives of the boys but when Jim called him, Michael walked over, standing beside him was Tom. Father Lafferty approached the three boys saying "Any of you boys want to go out? These people will bring you into the City for a look around", pointing to the man and woman beside him.

Three boys look at one another. Tom is the first to speak saying "You weren't out since you came here?"

"No" Michael replies.

"What about you Jim?" he asks.

"A couple from Clifden brought me out last year; I had a feed in the house."

Michael looks at the two people, wondering what is this all about. The old man holds his hands saying "Come on son, we can have a trip around Galway. You can go to the pictures if you want and we can have a feed some place. This is my wife Mary."

Holding her hand out to him she says "Young man."

Michael views the two people suspiciously but they seem alright. Tom and Jim stand looking at Michael. "Are you not coming lads?" he says.

"There was no one to take us." Jim replies.

"What about it?" Michael says looking at the old man.

"Alright," he says, "hop on the back and we will have a look around the City".

The three boys walk out the door towards the car, little knowing who the priest is that is watching them. Michael and his buddies are brought for a spin around Galway. The two old people are very nice; their son was killed in a car accident some time ago. The old man asked them what they would like to do. The boys replied "Maybe a film or a visit to the seaside and look at some seagulls."

The man answered them in a loud voice, "Now lads, the first thing is back to my place, there is a bit of turkey left over and we will see what happens then."

The man and wife bring them to their house and then they discover that they are in for a surprise. Going into the sitting room the woman brings out delph and lays it on the table. The man turns on the television, watching it for a while. Michael notices the piano in the corner. "Can you play that yoke in the corner?" Michael says.

"No," the man replies, "but my son played it before he died."

"Sorry," Michael says, "I better stay where I am."

"No, you will not." the man replied. "My wife teaches music, she will play something for you after the feed".

Three boys sit down on the couch. Michael asks "What is your name Sir?"

"James Smyth," the man says, "And this is my wife Mary, we had a son Seamus, he died some years ago. He was cycling outside when he got hit with a car; it was at Christmas time it happened."

The three boys moved towards the table where the woman served out some food, 'turkey and ham and brussel sprouts'. The boys tear into it. It tastes a lot better than the stuff at the orphanage. Michael looks at his two mates and smiles. They will be good friends for the rest of their lives. They are thankful that Michael brought them. The last time they were out was a pure disaster. A visit to a picture house and a feed from a take away afterwards. Tom and Jim smiled back at Michael while the man served some dessert. "We will have a spin around the city afterwards and a walk on the seashore, if it's not too cold." the man says lighting a cigarette. "I would also like to visit my son's grave if you lads don't mind?"

The woman asks the three boys out to the hallway and points to a small room at the end. "This is my son's room." she says opening the door. "We keep it like it was."

The room is very small, a three feet divan bed with a picture of Elvis Presley over it, all around there are pictures of David Cassidy and the Rolling Stones. In the corner is a small guitar.

"Can I look at it?" Michael asks.

"You can," the lady replies holding a hanky to her eyes, "but be careful, it was only varnished last week".

Michael picks it up and strums it. Handing it to Tom and Jim he says "Be careful."

The two boys hold it between them smiling. "Was he good?" Tom asks.

"My son, yes he was good." the lady says, "He got his guitar from a band man two years before he died."

Michael takes the guitar and hands it back to the lady. "If I ever get out of the big house" he says, "I will make use of it and who knows, maybe I will be as big as those boys on the wall."

The lady wipes her tears and smiles, "You have made my husband and me happy for Christmas. I would give it to you but the priest would not allow it."

"Don't worry" Michael says. "The caretaker is bringing one in next week on the QT. We will have to hide it somewhere."

The old man enters the room saying "First we will go to the graveyard to visit my son."

The three boys walk out the front door. Tom looks at Michael saying. "Ask him for a fag."

Michael says, "Please Sir, can we have a cigarette? I saw you with some of them in the car on the way over."

"Are you ready Mary?" he shouts from the front door.

"I am washing my hair." she shouts from the bathroom. "I won't be ready for an hour." she shouts.

"Here lads have some of these." he shouts, handing Michael ten Woodbines. The man turns on the radio while the boys sit down smoking the cigarettes. The three boys listen to the music, 'Slade' singing 'Merry Christmas'. They heard it from the caretaker van three weeks ago. The boys clapped their hands and hold one another in a circle and they start singing. They put their fags in the ashtrays and their voices echo around the room.

Mary leaves the bathroom, the towel on her head shouting "What's the matter, are you all drunk?"

"No," the husband replies, "the boys are letting off some steam before we go out."

The old man looks at the two boys dancing and moving their arms, thinking of his own young lad. If he was here with the guitar the craic would be mighty. Taking out his wallet he looks at his photograph. As the tears fall he says "Happy Christmas, son, Happy Christmas".

Michael picks up a cigarette and looks over at the old man thinking 'What is he crying about?' "Alright close it down." he says looking at the two boys.

Taking the hanky from his pocket, Michael says "We are sorry if we have upset you, Sir."

The three boys gather around him while he shows them the photograph. "He was a fine lad," Tom says.

"Yes," Jim says, "a fine lad."

"Come on," Michael says, "we will have to be going back shortly." Clapping the man on the back "It is time to move, come on."

As Mary comes out of the bathroom her husband holds her for a minute saying "They are good lads Mary, they are good lads."

As the boys tour the City, Michael notices a church. He remembers his father and mother years ago at his first communion and the day his mother bought the suit for him in some big shop in the City. A small tear formed in his eye as he thinks about her and his father. Looking at the two boys beside him he thinks 'What about the two boys?' "What are you thinking Jim?" he asks.

Jim smiles back at him saying "I don't know, Michael, It's nice to be out of that shithole." he says looking out the car window.

Tom moves over saying "My mam was never around for Christmas, it was just a card for me and my sister but dad always made us happy, he would always buy us Christmas presents and Christmas night he would be playing somewhere."

The three boys at the back put their hands around one another. Smiling Michael says "Happy Christmas lads, all the best for the future."

As the car turns towards the graveyard Mary turns around to the two boys saying "If you don't want to come in it's alright."

Michael looks at the boys saying "What do you think?"

"We will have a look around" Tom says.

Crossing over the wall the two people moved towards the right, then up the centre. Mary asked her husband to hold her hand saying "Boys wait here a minute, we won't be long". Tom and Jim sit down and look across the wall at the sea.

Michael sees a woman coming towards him. She is carrying rosary beads and stops just beside him. Reading the name on the headstone 'Tom Cribben died tragically at sea', no date. Michael looks at the lady and says "Your husband?"

"Yes," she replies, "there is no date because I feel he is still with me. I talk to him here once and week and at Christmas time when I am on my own in the house, I feel he is there with me. What's your name, young fellow?" she asks.

"Michael, Ma'am" he replies.

"Where do you live?" she asks.

"In an orphanage." he replies. "I am out for the day with those people over there."

The old lady looks at Michael and says "I have a young fellow like you, he is in America. If you feel like calling on me this is my address, bring your friends as well". Looking at the two boys at the wall she says "Goodbye and Happy Christmas."

Michael looks at the address and puts it in his pocket. 'Maybe someday', he thinks. Looking at the headstone in front of him he thinks of his mother's grave. 'It's been a long time' he thinks. 'I won't ask those people to go to the graveyard today, maybe next Christmas.' Holding his mother's medal in his hand he thinks 'maybe you are here today like that woman's husband.'

The old people beckoned him to come on, "It's time to be going", she says. "I told the priest you would be back at six o'clock."

Michael and his two mates walked back to the car. Sitting in the back seat he sees the old lady walking out the gate. "Who is that lady?" he asks.

"That's Mary," the man replies, "she comes down a few times a week, every time we visit our son's grave she is here, looking at the gravestone with no date, her husband was drowned at sea, the body was never found. Until the body is found she will never put a date on the tombstone. Your friend the priest objected to the stone but she got it up anyway."

'Sad' Michael thinks, 'very sad'.

The two people moved the car towards the City centre. "Lads I would bring you back for tea but you have to be back for six o'clock."

"That's, alright." Jim replies. "We had a great day, thanks. If you visit the orphanage you might bring a small radio or something like it. All the enjoyment we have is a bit of music."

Opening the dashboard, Mary takes out a small radio and hands it to him saying "Happy Christmas. You will have to get batteries but these will last a while."

Moving in the gates of the orphanage, Michael smiles "It wasn't a bad day after all, the only person missing was Dennis and he had went out with somebody else, we will see him tomorrow and show him the radio". The three boys waved goodbye to the visitors moving in the front door. Michael thinks 'Yes it was a pity Dennis wasn't with us but maybe the next time.'

During the next few days of Christmas nothing changed. School was called off until the 5th of January. Michael apologised to Dennis that he did not bring him on the trip. Dennis replied he would have gone if he was asked but he was not around at the time. Michael told him about the man and wife how the son died and he loved music, he also showed him the small radio. The next day himself, Tom, Jim and Dennis went to the back of the church to listen to it. The priest, Father Johnson was watching. Michael thought to himself 'you won't get this, we haven't much comfort in this hole, I will hide it somewhere where no one will get it'. Moving around the back of the orphanage Michael sees an old statue.

At the back of it is a small light with a hole underneath. Michael takes the transistor and puts it into it closing it over with some stones and a plastic bag to keep it dry. 'We will listen to you some other day,' he thinks, 'when the cowboy is not around.'

Chapter 8

The next day when Michael was cleaning the hallway, he noticed the caretaker fixing the lights in one of the rooms.

"Hello, big fellow." Michael shouts.

"Hello there Mr. Music man." he replies. "I have that guitar but these boys are very strict, if I'm bringing it in you will have to hide it somewhere."

"Where?" said Michael.

"There is a dungeon at the back of the church. I will show you later."

Michael rubs the floor with a mop, excited about the situation. The priest watches over him from upstairs. He did not hear the conversation but he could see the smile on Michael's face. Father Johnson did not like the look on Michael's face since he returned after Christmas. He had been visiting his mother and father in Dublin who both are old and retarded. After he returned a few days ago he noticed a smile on Michael's Tom and Jim's faces. He thought they might have been drinking or smoking. No, he checked with the people who brought them out. Michael notices the shadow as he cleans the floor. Looking up at him he thinks 'One of these days someone will kick you over the banisters, you white collared ass.' As Michael takes the bucket and mop and puts them in the spare room, Father Johnson walks up and down leaving a track on the wet floor.

"You made a bad job of this, you little pup." he says.

"It's alright if it is left alone." Michael said.

"Don't give me any cheek, get out that mop and clean it."

"It's six o' clock." Michael said. "I have to get something to eat."

Just as Michael is about to take his bucket from the closet, Father Lafferty walks down the corridor.

"What's wrong young man? You should be having some food." Michael points to the other priest. "Its 6 o'clock its time this lad had something to eat." he shouts at the priest.

Father Johnson shouts back "The floor is wet."

"It's not wet, it's damp, get lost." Father Lafferty says. "Go and get something to eat, I have to talk about choir practice later on."

Michael goes down to the kitchen. Jim, Tom and Dennis are sitting down eating. "You are very late," Jim says "what's wrong?"

"The two white collared boys delayed me a bit. How are things?" Michael asks.

"Not too bad," Jim says, "Dennis got a few belts of the hand from Johnson. He can hardly use his left hand."

"Show me." Michael says. As he looks at his hand he says "You want to wash it with something. Come on down to the toilet I have Dettol down there. Keep an eye on the grub till we come back, lads." he says.

Michael and Dennis walked into the bathroom. Dennis holds his hand under the tap while Michael puts some Dettol in the water.

"What's going on here?" a voice says. It's Father Johnson sticking his head in the door.

"You hurt this fellow's hand." Michael says.

"I will do more than hurt his hand if he does not do what he is told."

"Come on Dennis," Michael says "we better get back; we will get something for this after a while."

Michael and Dennis moved back to the kitchen. Opening the cabinet, he takes a box of cotton wool and rubs it on his sore hand. "We won't put any plaster on it." he says, "It will heal itself. What did he hit you for?" Michael asks.

"Myself and Tom were singing at the back of the church, the caretaker had the radio on."

As Michael and his mate move up the hallway he thinks 'Some of you white collar boys would want to watch yourselves, that big ass Johnson will hit somebody yet and somebody will return the belt.' "Maybe me," Michael says "Maybe me," holding his fist out. The boys move back to their rooms and he thinks 'I wonder if the radio is alright.' Moving around in the bed he thinks about the music he heard on it. It was an English group by the name of 'The Who'. Touching his head back on the pillow he moves his fingers as if playing a guitar. Smiling he thinks 'They are a good band.' The smile is still on his face ten minutes afterwards when he is asleep.

Matt Doyle

Chapter 9

Michael wakes next morning to the sound of the lawn mower in the garden. The room is full of kids, some young, some not so young. Michael is fourteen now, his life is changed. Looking out the window he sees the birds in the lawn and the caretaker collecting leaves. Michael's thinking is disturbed by the sound of a priest Father O'Malley. "Hurry it up, lads," he says, "football at 3 o'clock, choir practice at 5 o'clock."

As Michael walks to the kitchen he sees Dennis standing in the corner. "What's wrong?" he asks.

"Nothing," he replies, "just thinking about something."

"What is the matter?" Michael shouts, "You look very down."

"I am alright." Dennis replies. "I was just looking at my father's photograph, this morning. What is going to come of us Michael?" he says staring into his eyes. "Are we going to live like normal people again or are we going to die in this shithole?"

"We are going to get out of here," Michael says, "in a few years time. You, me and the other two lads, we will start a band and we will become famous. Now, dry your eyes with this." he says giving him a tissue.

"Maybe," Dennis replies, "I still think you are dreaming."

Michael puts his hand around him saying "You like music, I like music, Jim and Tom like music, that's all we have, no parents but music and that's not bad Dennis." he says.

The two boys put their hands around one another and walked towards the kitchen. Two smiles back on their faces. Lonely, but not alone. The four feet moved to the sound of humming. What the song is they don't know. "Who cares," Michael smiles "it's still good music."

The classes changed in the next few months, Michael is sent to the gardens and the fields. Jim is sent to the woodwork room where he learns to make tables and chairs or repair existing ones. The orphanage is self sufficient, the vegetables from the fields, the milk from the dairy cows, hens and ducks are also reared for food. Where the milk came from no one ever knew because there was always a bad taste off it. There were two sheds away from the orphanage where pigs were reared; the bacon was usually fairly good. Dennis and Tom knew a few of the dairy girls who milked the cows. These girls were from a convent nearby. Nobody knew much about them but the boys would get cigarettes off them sometimes. They hid them in a dustbin at the back of the church. On a Sunday afternoon Michael would go to the back of the church and hide behind the hedge to listen to the music. The radio they got wasn't great; there was a lot of interference. One evening, as he was washing the soil off his hands, he thought it would be nice if one of the boys could make up a guitar in the workroom. Maybe this caretaker could get us a few strings. He had told Michael a few days before he had the guitar but he would have to leave it in the van, otherwise he could lose his job. Walking around the back of the building, he sees the caretaker sitting in the van. Looking into the vehicle he sees a small guitar. "Is this yours?" he asks.

"It is." the caretaker replies. "Sometimes when I am on my own I strum a bit, it gives me a bit of a lift. This job of mine gets rather monotonous sometimes."

Michael lifts up the guitar, strumming he says "My fingers are very big."

"Not as big as mine." the caretaker replies. "Show me the guitar." he says. Michael hands it back to him. Moving his fingers up and down the frets, he hums the tune.

The movement of the guitar and the humming brings a smile to Michael's face. "What do they call that?" he asks.

"It's called 'Singing the Blues'." he replies. "Here, hold it young fellow and stick your fingers on the strings I'll show you. When you start humming, do the strumming as I did." Michael holds the guitar and puts his fingers heavy on the strings. The caretaker shouts "Don't make a mess of it."

Michael looks at him and thinks 'You have a problem lad; you think you are something.'

"Sorry for shouting. You want to play music, yes? Just do as I say, hold the guitar like this and strum these two chords." Michael takes the guitar and strums the way the caretaker shows him. "That's better," he says "the guitar is like a woman, you have to rub it the right way, strum them two chords and I will sing and keep time, with you." The caretaker starts singing; he nods to Michael to start strumming. Singing, the caretaker similes over at him. "That's good, young lad," he says, "that's good." Finishing this song he looks at his watch and says "You better get going or I will get the bullet out of here."

"See you soon." Michael says handing him back the guitar.

"Hurry on young man." he replies. Michael walks back towards the kitchen to his room. The caretaker casts his eyes at him as he walks away. Rubbing his face he thinks 'that young lad has talent, I only hope he gets a chance to use it.'

Michael returned to his room that night thinking about the man with the guitar 'By God' he thinks, 'he is good, that bloke's music was cool and with the way he played it. If only Jim could make up some guitar and put some sort of music together maybe we could start somewhere.' Michael lies back on the bed looking up at the ceiling he thinks 'By God that caretaker is good.'

He is awoken the next morning to the sound of rain and wind. The sound of doors banging, everyone rushing all around the place.

Jumping out of the bed, Michael meets a young fellow in the hallway. "What's wrong?" he asks.

"Fire," the young man says "down below."

Michael noticed the smoke coming from the corridor. "Who is down there?" he asks the young person.

"I don't know," he says "but whoever it is is in trouble." Michael grabs a hanky and moves down the stairs the smoke blocking his eyesight. "Who is down there?" he shouts.

"It's Jim." he replies. "It's Jim. There is an electrical fault in the laundry room, the shirts caught fire, hurry up Michael," he shouts, "I can hardly breathe."

Michael gets a hold of him and slowly carries him up the stairs as they reach the top, Michael feels dizzy and falls down the stairs. As he reaches the bottom he sees a hand through the smoke, it's the caretaker. Lifting Michael up on his shoulders he carries him up the stairs. The two of them rush outside for a breath of fresh air.

"What the hell were you doing down there?" he says to Michael.

"Jim was stuck down in the laundry room; I had to get him out."

"It's alright," a Priest says, "it was an electrical fault. It's a good job you got Jim out." he says to Michael. He never said thanks to the caretaker, it was as if he didn't exist.

Rumour had it around the place that the caretaker and some of the priests didn't get on but they couldn't get rid of him he was there that long. Michael walks out on the lawn coughing. Watching the smoke coming out of the bottom windows. "Are you alright Jim?" he says

"Not too bad." he says rubbing his eyes. "I owe you one buddy." he says to Michael. "That faulty plug sent the whole place up, I was nearly burned alive, all over bad electricity. If I had my hand in the sink, I would be dead."

The caretaker comes over, white with coughing. The Priest shouts at him "What happened down there, what happened?"

"The electricity down there was faulty this last two years" the caretaker says.

Father Johnson shouts at the man "Shut up."

"I will shut you up you idiot, these two boys were nearly burned alive, all though your negligence."

The argument is interrupted by Father Lafferty. "Alright you two, take it easy." He points to the caretaker saying "Close it off and take out the fuses, we will look at it tomorrow."

"What about the laundry?" Father Johnson says. "The clothes will be alright for a while," he says, "until we get the electricity working properly. Anyway, they won't rot for a week or two and the kitchen sink and carbolic soap can do a lot."

Michael goes to the back of the building and looks up at the sky. 'Lucky I didn't suffocate in there.' he thinks.

He sees the two boys coming towards him Jim and Tom. "How are you feeling buck?" Jim asks.

"Not too bad lads." he replies. "We have to get together sometime and see what happens with the music."

"I know, but what about the instruments at the back of the church?" Jim says. "Meet at nine o' clock, we will talk then and see what happens."

As Michael cleans the kitchen that night he notices Father Lafferty and Father Johnson arguing outside.

"It was a bad wire connection." Father Lafferty shouts.

"It was that young pup," Father Johnson replies, "he was messing around with it."

"Leave him alone or you will be sorry." Lafferty says.

"I am here a long time." Johnson says.

"You will not be here much longer if you don't leave those kids alone. You will find yourself somewhere else the Priest argues."

Father Johnson holds his head down; he knows the other priest is right. One word from the Bishop and he could find himself out in Africa. He had been there as a young priest but never again. He still had nightmares over what he saw out there. Johnson walks away, talking to himself.

Father Lafferty walks into the kitchen his face red with temper. "Good night Michael," he says, "when you have cleaned up the place put out the light."

As Michael finishes his job he sees two boys standing outside the window. Jim and Tom, standing beside them there is someone else in the shadow. "Who is that behind you?" he asks opening the window. Coming out of the shadow he sees it is Dennis.

"What are we going to do here?" Dennis asks. "Tom asked me over here, this evening."

The four boys move towards the back of the church. Michael says to Jim "If we are caught the white collar boys will lead us to the cross."

Jim replies "Who cares. We cannot live with this shit all the time. We were left here alone, no parents, no relatives; the only fun we have is a bit of music."

"Your right," Michael replies, "if we are caught, we are caught".

The four boys moved towards the van at the back of the building. Sitting inside it is the caretaker strumming his guitar. The four boys stand looking at him smiling. He is about their only salvation in this place. Looking into the van the four boys notice that he has loudspeakers on and he is singing very slowly. He does not see the boys as the lights outside the church are very low. Michael stands back looking at him a small tear in his eyes. Watching him playing and singing, moving his fingers and changing chords he thinks he must get a book of chords and learn them. If ever the boys could make up a guitar, something simple, he might get time to practice on it. 'We will see what the caretaker says' he thinks.

The caretaker moves his eyes slowly looking out of the van. He does not recognise the boys with the darkness. "Who is there?" he shouts.

"It's us." Michael shouts back.

"I thought you would be here earlier, if the white collar boys find you, you will be in big trouble, its ten o'clock I was expecting you at seven."

"If they find out, what about?" Michael says. "All we have in this place is at the back of this van. No family, no friends, bad food, the only bit of happiness around here is you and your music."

"Lads, I work here, I have a job to do, a few years time you will be gone into that world out there. The fire that started today, did you tell them how it happened Jim?"

Jim smiled at Michael "No." he says.

"Myself and Jim were trying out one of my guitars and the whole bloody place nearly went up."

"What about," Jim replies, "it was worth it for the craic."

Michael looks back at him saying "Some craic, if some of the strings got wet you would be toasted."

"Come in here you four cowboys and sit down." he says "I will show you some of the chords associated with the guitar. Michael, I talked to you before, get a pen and paper and sit down. Take hold of that guitar Michael and I will show you some of the major chords. No loud noise lads. If it is loud the white collar boys will start roving." Pointing at Jim, "There is a small drum beside you," he says, "when I say so just drum one two, one two". The four boys sit down in the middle of the van. Dennis picks up the double drum and starts thumping it. "Quiet," the caretaker says "while I shut the door".

Michael picks up the guitar and strums it. Tom picks up the other one. "What is the difference?" Tom asks the caretaker.

"That's a base guitar you have, Michael's is a lead guitar. I would plug them in but it would be too noisy. Michael, you strum up and down," he says, "Tom just strum down, don't mess it up." The caretaker moves his hands on the chords, "Follow that." he says to Michael. "You follow this one." he says to Tom. "That's it," he says "that's it, practice that." Dennis beat the drum, one, two, one, two. "Jim, put this in your mouth it's a mouth organ, just do this ok?" The caretaker moves it over his mouth making a blues sound. The caretaker strums the guitar slowly humming a tune.

"What's the name of that one?" Michael asks.

"Shut up and watch my fingers." he replies.

Michael thinks 'You are rather loud, but if I am going to learn music it's not going to sound good all the time'.

Tom moves his finger down on the base guitar. Michael watches the teacher moving his right hand up and down the guitar. Dennis beats the tom tom and Jim blows the mouth organ over and back in the mouth. The small van slowly comes alive to the sounds of the music, each trying to reach for the perfect sound. Their faces red with excitement. Tears forming in their eyes. This is their heaven; the place they live in is hell. They forget they are orphans, forget they have no parents, they forget the white collar boys and when they pray in the church or at night time beside the bed they thank God for their music and the caretaker who is giving them the only happiness they know.

Later that night, as the boys returned to their room to their beds, they did not note but they were being watched by someone at the top window, Father Johnson.

As Michael pulls the blankets over him, he looks at the ceiling. Moving his fingers ever so slowly, he watches their shadow on the ceiling. He is playing the chord d̲ like the caretaker taught him. Smiling, it looks like a turkey on the ceiling. 'Strange,' Michael thinks, 'there is only one chord but now it's a̲ and g. It makes the guitar sound good.' Looking at his mother's medal he kisses it and goes to sleep. He does not hear himself but he is humming the song 'Me and Bobby McGee', the song the caretaker played tonight.

Michael awakens early next morning to the sound of an argument. Jumping out of the bed he runs to the top of the stairs. Father Johnson is using a ruler on one of the boys, Dennis.

"You English tramp." he shouts at him, hitting him across the ear. "You and your buddies were missing from the room last night, I will give you music." he shouts, hitting him with the ruler across the hand.

"Leave him alone," Michael shouts down at him, "you white collared ass."

The Priest looks up the stairs at Michael shouting, "I will be with you in a minute you little pup." He throws Dennis to the ground and starts climbing the stairs. As he walks into the room Michael hides under the bed. "Come out wherever you are," he shouts, "I will teach you some manners." Michael stays under the bed shaking. The Priest goes over to the window and opens it a bit more. Looking out he wonders if Michael has hidden under the ledge. What he does not see is the shadow behind him.

Tom moves ever so slowly, lifting him by the shoes he shouts "Have a right look."

The Priest shouts "Stop, stop", it's too late. Tom's strength when he grabs his feet leaves the Priest shouting for help as he hangs on to the ledge. "Help me please, help me, it's a long drop." he shouts.

Tom looks into the priest's eyes and says "Don't worry you won't be going to heaven. Goodbye." he says as he puts his boot on the priest's hands. "Goodbye." he says again and the priest falls to the ground.

"Disappear Tom," Michael shouts, "we will have the law up here shortly."

"Are you alright Michael?" Tom Shouts.

"I am sound, just move fast and say nothing, Dennis is downstairs."

Within minutes there are panic stations outside the buildings. Father O'Malley and Father Lafferty rush into the room shouting "What happened?"

"I don't know," Michael shouts, "he must have slipped near the window and fell out."

"Call an ambulance," Father Lafferty says, "and don't move him till it comes." Father O'Malley moves down the stairs to the phone. All the boys are outside looking down on him. No tears, no pity. If he asks for a drink of water he would not get it.

The Priest is unconscious on the ground as the ambulance moves onto the lawn. A doctor examines him. "How is he?" Father O'Malley asks. "Is there any broken bones?" The two men don't answer him. All they do is lift him up onto the stretcher and put him into the ambulance.

Jim looks at Michael and says "When they get him to the hospital they might put him in a straight jacket." Michael does not laugh. There will be an inquiry and there will be questions asked. Father Johnson did never return to the orphanage, it was heard afterwards that he developed amnesia. There was an inquiry but it was put down to an accident.

Jim heard the story from the caretaker. When he was talking to Michael later on he said "Small loss for what he did to that boy Dennis."

Two weeks later, a priest arrived from County Cavan; his name was Father Leonard, a young man only out of Maynooth a short time. The first week he did a lot of inspection around the place. A very tiny man, he kept the kitchen in order and checked the boy's room every day for cleanliness. Michael worked with him sometimes in the kitchen and if he did his job properly he would offer him some rhubarb and custard from the fridge. The rhubarb was growing at the back of the garden and Michael would watch him as he made rhubarb tarts.

It was during this period that an old woman started visiting the place. She would come in sometimes and bring some rhubarb tarts with her. Michael thought he recognised her from somewhere and it was only after a long time he realised she was the caretaker's mother and it was the photograph in the van where he recognised her. Michael would sometimes come in at night after cleaning the floor and sit in the kitchen for a while. He would see the pair of them outside the window talking. It was later he heard that the lady adopted him and that he was an orphan himself in the place. Her name was Ruth.

Michael heard the story from Father O'Malley who was a long time priest in the place. He told him when he was practising the organ in the church. Michael never liked the organ it was the singing that appealed to him.

A few days later when he was cleaning the floors he noticed her sitting at the table. "Fancy a cup of tea?" she asks him.

"I am not supposed to be in here." he says, "I am supposed to eat in the main room with the other boys."

"Sit down." she shouts at him, "If anybody says anything I will talk to them, I am only here for a short time, the Bishop sent me over here to clean the place up a bit."

"You and the caretaker are good friends." Michael says with a shake in his hands.

"We are." she replies putting the tea in front of him. "Put in the milk and sugar yourself." she says.

Michael drinks the tea thinking 'This is a lot better than the bog water I get in the other place.'

"The caretaker's name is Martin Collins. I adopted him some years ago. He was deserted by his father and mother when he was very young. He saw some rough times here speaking with a Dublin accent. His uncle was a priest, I kept house for him for years, he was sent to this orphanage at an early age. His uncle made sure he was looked after by the clergy and that he got a fair shot at life." Lighting a cigarette she looks at Michael saying "You are just one of many that passed through here. I was not allowed around this place till lately. Martin stays with me all the time, I am like his mother. It is only lately that I am allowed to visit him here, why I don't know."

'It must be over that Johnson priest leaving.' Michael thinks.

"I bring him sandwiches on a Sunday; he is alright when he has his music. He told me some time ago that the boys were good at music. We were talking the other night at home and he told me that you and the other boys played at the back of the van, is that right?" She asked.

"It is," Michael replies, "and if we ever get out of this place we might start something together".

"There is no future in music lad." she says lighting another cigarette. "I told him too but he would not listen. That van of his is like a castle; he sleeps in it with the music on. He plays it in different pubs in Galway and Mayo. He gets small money but it covers him for grub and petrol. Sometimes he brings the Alsatian for company. Someone tried to break in one night to his van to steal his guitar and the dog caught his arm. My man says he would not play the guitar for a while anyway."

Michael listens intently with wide eyes and a big smile on his face. Thinking 'If ever I get out of this place I will do the same thing.'

His dreams are disturbed by the sound of footsteps in the hall. Two priests, Father Lafferty and Father O'Malley.

Looking into the kitchen one of the priest shouts "What are you doing there young fellow?"

"What do you mean," The lady replies, "talking to me."

"We know that Mary but Michael is wanted up there at the altar he has to do his bit. You are singing in the choir Michael" Father O'Malley says. "We have a guest today from America, some friend of the Bishop. He likes singing and promised a new organ for the church."

"Do the best you can Michael" Father Lafferty says.

Michael holds his hands out to the lady to say goodbye a small tear in his eye. The soft skin reminds him of his mother years ago. The lady looks at him saying "Don't worry lad, things will work out. Music is strange," she says, "you never have it and you never lose it. See you later on." she says rubbing her fingers through his hair.

Chapter 10

As Michael climbs the balcony he sees his mates Jim, Tom and Dennis. "Where have you been, buck?" Jim says.

"Talking to a lady," he replies, "the caretaker's mother."

"We were going to have a bit of music out the back, but we are not much good on our own." Said Jim.

"I am sorry lads, I have to go upstairs and sing some choir music, you might as well come up and join in."

As Michael opens the door he sees Father O'Malley at the organ. "It's not working too good." he says.

"It's alright," Michael says, "me and these boys will shade it out a bit."

Father O'Malley replies "He is sitting up at the altar, the Bishop; if we do this lads we might get a new organ. We are looking for one for this last five years."

Michael thinks to himself 'It would be better if we got a few guitars not that 'pile of shit.'

The Bishop looks up at the boys. Father O'Malley waves back at him and says "Boys, form a straight line will you? When I play don't sing till I repeat the first verse on the organ."

Michael, Jim, Tom and Dennis stand behind the priest smiling. Some of the other lads sit in front of them. Michael casts a glance over the stairs and sees the caretaker leaning against the wall. Michael smiles over at him and he waves back. Father O'Malley shouts over at him saying "You are not part of the choir."

Michael says "Leave him alone, he is our friend."

"Alright," the Priest says, "but he should not be up here". The priest starts playing very slowly. Watching the Bishop and his friend from America. Second time around, Michael starts to sing 'Amazing Grace.' As the organ takes over, Jim starts to hum while Michael and his buddies sing. Eventually the organ is drowned out by the singing and humming of the four boys. Father O'Malley is not too impressed but he cannot say a lot. The Bishop sits at the side of the church with the priest while one of them says Mass. There is another man up in the front seat. Every so often he looks up at the balcony. His looks change from a frown to a smile as Michael's singing takes over. Thinking about what the priest said Michael keeps an eye on him thinking 'We might get something else off this yank, a car would be handy.'

Father O'Malley looks over at Michael with a frown. Michael knows he is in for it now. "You made a mess of it, young fellow." he says. "What am I going to tell the Bishop? Its choir music we want not some soaped up bullshit. You will remain in your room for the rest of the day with no dinner; you will get down the stairs fast."

Michael sings to himself as he walks down the stairs "I don't give a shit I enjoyed it."

Looking at the caretaker Michael shakes his hand, "You're in big trouble, now my man, that was the Bishop down there. He will want an explanation." the caretaker says smiling.

As Michael reaches the bottom of the stairs, six priests glare at him with disgust. Their eyes are pevious and they are all wearing glasses. The silence is broken by a loud voice. "Hi, you man, are you the singer?"

"One of them," Michael replies in a sarcastic voice, "who are you?" Michael asks.

"I am related to the big boy up there," pointing to the Bishop up at the altar. "I have not great time for this religious baloney, but you and the boys have got a bit of talent."

'Bullshit,' Michael thinks 'big mouth, no action. You would want to tell that to the white collar boy upstairs, he said we were only a pile of shit.'

"Less of your tongue, young man" a priest says looking at him. "You would want to learn a bit of respect, you know damn well it's not church music you were singing. What sort of a sick boy are you?" raising his hand to hit him.

"Hold it big fellow." the yank shouts. "I liked the music and the way they sang it."

Father O'Malley walks over saying "Sorry Sir, this boy is going to be remanded for his behaviour."

"Over my dead body. Come down here," he shouts at the Bishop, "and hurry up."

The Bishop replied, "This is a church not a dance hall."

"But it should be," the yank shouts, "The acoustics are excellent. I recorded music in Nashville and it did not sound half as good as what went on upstairs."

"Make your point." the Bishop says.

"Alright Uncle Jim."

Father O'Malley intervenes saying, "You are related to the Bishop?"

"Sure," the yank replies, "he is my uncle, I haven't seen him for years. He said he wanted a donation for this place and I said alright."

"He is right," the Bishop replies, "he is my brother's son home from Nashville and I told him about the organ upstairs and he asked me to get someone to play it. I told him it was in bad shape but he still wanted to hear it. These musicians are funny people." the Bishop says looking at the priests.

"What do you want?" the yank says "A new organ uncle? I run the show here for the next hour or you keep that old box upstairs".

The priest stared thinking 'Alright.' Father O'Malley shouts, "Let him run the show for a while and see what happens."

Another priest says "You have got to remember you are in a church and you just cannot treat it like a dancehall."

"I know," the yank replies, "we will go out the back, there is a building beside the main gate. I will get my guitar and you boys can help me with the recording."

Michael asks him, "Can we include an old friend in the recording?" he says pointing to the top of the stairs.

"He is a bit old." the yank says.

"He is our friend and a good musician."

"This is not church policy," the Bishop says, "It will give this place a bad name."

"My father and you are brothers and music is good for the soul." the yank says.

"Alright big fellow," the Bishop replies, "but these boys could be in trouble after we go. The priests have rules and regulations which I have no control over, no priest likes his authority questioned nephew." the Bishop says in a strong voice.

"Look, you white collar boys," the yank says, "I am impressed with these boys, their voices are very good. If you want a new organ you have it. You should do it my way or you will keep your pile of junk upstairs."

The priest looked over at the Bishop. "Don't look at me." he shouts. "Do you want a new organ or do you not? If not, we will go home. He is a high class musician in Nashville and he has money. I cannot give you any money."

Michael looks over at the priest thinking 'You are a funny lot'.

"Alright," Father O'Malley says, "you can sing Michael along with Jim, Tom and Dennis but, the caretaker, no."

"If he doesn't sing and play, we don't." Michael says.

"Watch your manners boy; I am the boss man here, not the man with the pony tail."

Michael talks to the yank quietly. The yank goes back to the Bishop and says "If the pony tail boy doesn't play there is no organ. If he does, you will have your money before Easter cost what it may."

The priests talk together for a short while. Father Lafferty approaches the yank saying "We have rules here son, it's not the organ, we have rules. If this conversation ever broke out about the music and the organ, it's not the

Bishop, it's not you, and it's not the rest of the boys with the collars on."

The yank brushes him aside saying to the caretaker, "If you have an instrument get it, if you four lads follow me I will organise something."

"Congregate at the back of the hall and not a word about this," says the priest, "or it could make things very ugly for everybody."

Chapter 11

All the priests, the Bishop and the orphans congregate at the back hall. Michael, Jim, Tom and Dennis sit on the stage when the caretaker sets up the instruments. Two guitars, one set of drums. The caretaker brings his instruments from the back of the van. "A fiddle, I will play this while the Yankee boy plays the guitar."

Michael says "Have you an extra one of those?" pointing to the guitar on the stage.

"Here, take this one." the caretaker says. "Break the strings and I will kill you, it belongs to my mother."

A large crowd of children sit down in front of the stage, no chairs just cross their legs while the priests sit around with stern faces, the Bishop in the middle.

"Hurry up." the yank shouts at the musicians. "This uncle of mine wants to get this music finished as quickly as possible in case it causes a scandal."

Michael and his three mates stand at the back. The caretaker fires three chairs in front of them. "You Jim play this, it is a damaged drum but it will sound alright, Michael you play the guitar. Dennis, see what you can do with this tambourine. Tom, stand back and give us a bit of backing." As the boys take their positions the hall slowly fills up with young people. Some smiling, some suspicious of the whole situation.

The yank talks to one of the priests saying "Get some orange and biscuits out there for the kids and hot tea and sandwiches on the stage for the band." The four boys stand at the back of the stage looking at the big crowd. Michael is nervous with the whole situation. 'God help them' he thinks, 'they haven't seen much in this dive. Some of these kids seem lost, no parents, no guardians. What about,' he thinks, 'this music should put a sparkle back in their lives only if it's for 50 minutes or an hour.'

"This is highly irregular." says one of the priests.

"Maybe," the Bishop replies, "but my nephew wants to play with these young boys, but maybe, you never know, something good could come out of it."

The yank stands on the stage while the caretaker strums his guitar. "How are you feeling, big man?" the yank asks.

"Not too bad, Yankee boy." he replies.

The four boys stand behind him all looking down at the ground. The caretaker says to the boys "You know the song we played last year at the back of the church?"

"I do," Michael says, "but I don't know the name of it but it sure had a nice rhythm."

"It sounds like this Yankee boy." the caretaker says strumming his guitar.

"I know," the yank replies, "it is the Beach Boy's rhythm, alright let's hum it." he says. The yank shouts down at the crowd "Are you ready for the music down there? Then let's see you clap your hands." Clapping his hands over his head he shouts, "Let's see those hands."

The faces of the orphans light up their white teeth smiling with joy. The room comes alive the sound of clapping and laughter. The yank strums his guitar while the caretaker backs him. Michael hums the tune while the three boys move ever so slightly to the left and then to the right. The yank opens with the word "Surfing" and the three boys repeat it. The caretaker strums his guitar along with Michael. Suddenly all the music stops and hands take over. The yank shouts down at the crowd "Come on, let's see those hands." The whole room comes alive with clapping and laughter.

The only people with stern faces are the priests and the Bishop. "This is highly irregular", Father O'Malley says to the Bishop, "highly irregular."

"Maybe."

Father O'Malley smiles back at him. 'Maybe I wasted my time with this job.' he thinks. 'Maybe if things were different I might be up there along with that big yank. I sometimes wish I joined that big band with my brother years ago but I am quite happy where I am now.' Looking up at the boys he thinks 'you have it lads, you have it. Anyway when we get the organ', the Priest thinks, 'all the self pity will disappear.'

As the music stops everybody claps. The orphans head for the table for orange and biscuits. The lads move off the stage to the table in front of them. Michael drinks his tea and holds his hand out to Jim, Tom and Dennis. Leaving the cups down the four boys put their arms around one another, crying. "We have been a long time in this kip." Michael says. "We have had some hard times, what about." he says. "The music is ours and ours alone."

The yank looks down at the four boys smiling. 'Those poor lads are good and very good." he thinks. Holding his hand out to the caretaker he says "Big fellow, you made a good job of those lads."

"No one is supposed to know that." he replies. "If the white collar boys found out we would be in serious trouble."

"Don't worry," the yank says, "this organ will keep them quiet. Give me your address, I will write to you from the States." he says. "Who knows, if those boys ever get out I may be able to do something for them."

"Alright nephew," the Bishop says walking over to him, "you have had your fun, let's go over to my place. These men of the cloth are hard come by. I have a job to do," he says, "and working with the Church is not the easiest job in the world."

"Don't worry uncle," he replies, "they will have their organ and a good one it will be."

The room clears out slowly, the priests faces solemn, not too happy with the way the day went. Their authority was threatened by the Yankee boy. Michael watches from the stage and thinks 'What about to see the young kids leaving humming the music. It was well worth it to see the smiles on their faces.' He looks back at the caretaker and says "Thanks bud; we didn't do so bad, myself and the boys."

Jim smiles up at him and says "It was the best day we enjoyed since we came to this dump."

Jumping down off the stage Jim, Michael, Tom and Dennis walk out of the door humming a tune by the 'Beach Boys' as they walk out into the yard. The caretaker smiles down at him and says "It's been a pleasure lads, and you are about the best thing that happened in my life since I started working here."

The organ did arrive shortly afterwards.

Chapter 12

The smile on the priests faces showed what happened a week before was forgotten about. It was carried up the stairs the following Sunday. The sound of it could be heard outside the walls of the establishment. Michael and his three buddies were not too impressed. Their taste in music had changed. Choir music was not their style. The caretaker still taught the boys out the back at night time but he was not himself lately. Michael asked him "What is wrong Mr Guitar man?"

He smiled back at him saying "Nothing Michael, nothing. Just stay with the music lads, don't worry about me."

It was during the next year that the boy's music took off. Michael and the caretaker, Jim, Tom and Dennis were put in different parts of the orphanage but they all met at the back of the van after 12 o'clock. Time moved on slowly. Hard work in the fields. Michael cleaning the floors. Jim and Tom doing the laundry in the evening.

Dennis worked mostly in the kitchen. Some of the other boys were let go about around the City. A lot of them were there because the parents were in England and their relatives would bring them out every now and again for the Easter. Nobody ever called for the boys. They talked among themselves and they had no one they knew about. It was at this period that they talked to the caretaker one night and they decided they had to escape but 'where to' Michael wondered, 'where to.'

The caretaker looked at them from afar and thought 'where to is right. If they were caught outside these walls they would be sent to a rougher place. If they were caught in Ireland they might never see the outside world for ten years. They were cheap labour for the clergy. A lot of hotels got their food cheap and their laundry was done as well. Nobody cared.' he thought. 'They were in here for the good of society but society didn't ask any questions. Life on the outside just went on and on the inside these boys were numbers.'

They were sixteen now and Michael was seventeen. They would probably get work outside but separate them and they were lost. They played together; they cried together, they fought together, they were brothers through the music. Take them away from the music and separate them, they would probably die and get lost on the outside in some bad place or in some bad company. They were inseparable and the only one that new that was the caretaker. He was their God, heaven and their only salvation from the shit that was all around them. He knew they were all good musicians, he knew their music was worth something. Not only to themselves, but to the people in the orphanage. He saw the way the other kids talked to them, smiled at them. They were four good-looking fellows; talented, rich with enthusiasm for the outside world but, if they were separated or adopted by different people the music would die. They would become judges of their own talent and so would other people. If that happened they would lose interest in life and wind up on the streets. Bums with guitars. Street bums with a better talent that Elvis Presley. The caretaker lights a cigarette and thinks. Blowing the smoke up the air he talks to himself saying "No way baby it is not going to happen, no way."

The four boys meet the next day in the laundry room. Michael and Tom sit down in the corner on an old sack. Jim and Dennis stand looking at them. "This caretaker friend of ours is worried a bit. I think something is going to happen." Michael says. "Rumour has it they are going to shift him out of here shortly. If he goes the music goes, we will be lost. He is our only link to the outside world."

"I think," Jim replies "they will separate us maybe, send you to Dublin Dennis and me somewhere else."

"I don't know," Michael replies, "but I get the feeling things are going to change around here".

"What makes you think that Michael?" asks Jim.

"I heard some talk in the kitchen." Michael says. "The priest and some young orphan reckon they can do the caretaker's job. The buck does not know it yet."

"That lady you were talking to in the kitchen some time ago, she might know something?" Tom says.

"I doubt it," Michael says, "but if we are going to get out of here we will have to move in the next year. If we get split up they have no papers on us and we have no contact outside this dump. We will probably be leaving within a year or two, but all at different times. Maybe some old farmer or somebody will adopt us for donkey work, no pay and no respect for our talent."

The four boys move out to the centre of the yard. Putting their hands around one another Michael says "We will go together lads, we will start a band somewhere and we will stay together through thick and thin." They huddled together, the word 'band' bringing tears to their eyes.

Chapter 13

It's later that evening when Michael is cleaning the hall that he meets the caretaker. The caretaker sits in the kitchen along with the lady. "What are you staring at?" he says to Michael.

"Sorry," he replies, "I was thinking about something that is all."

"I am sorry Mr big man. You heard the news I suppose that I was leaving?" he says.

"We heard it." Michael says. "If you go we will be lost."

"You will not." the caretaker shouts. "I cannot stay here all the time. You know how things are; sometimes you have to move on. I play a bit of music, I can do handy work around the City." he says, staring down at the coffee.

Michael looks at him, knowing he is burning up inside. He likes the boys. He taught them some good music and Michael and his mates played with him. It brought a shine to his hair and a smile to his face. Michael goes over to the table. The lady gets up and walks away. Holding out his hands to the caretaker he says "If you go we will go as well."

"Your crazy." he replies. "If you are caught you will be send to a worse place, maybe Dublin or Belfast and you won't be together, you will never see one another again. No relatives, no family, just a name on a bit of paper and maybe a wrong name at that. Wait another two years." he says looking at the young man in front of him. "You will get your freedom and then you will be together."

"No," Michael says, "If you go we all go."

The woman walks back into the room smoking a cigarette. Looking at the caretaker she says "The boys are adamant you will have to help them."

"What ages are they?" he said looking up at her.

"It does not matter about age, only you and me can help them. You gave them your music. The chances are they will be split up in the next few years. If you help them now, they will stay together as friends and musicians."

"I am not the law." the caretaker shouts. "If they walk out of here with me where are they going to stay, who will look after them? I have no money and it's no good bringing them around the country playing music. The law would be on them hot and heavy."

"You have a brother in Spain, haven't you?" she replies.

"You're crazy woman." he shouts at her. "How are we going to get four orphans out to Spain? No passports, no identity cards, no family or relatives. My brother owns a night club out there, what are these boys going to do, play music in it?"

"Why not?" the woman shouts at him. "He escaped from an orphanage years ago; he would be able to look after them."

The caretaker looks behind and sees the other boys standing beside Michael. They came in unknown to him. They all looked down at the ground with sad faces. She is right, he knows she is right. Split them up and they will be lost. "All right lady, see what you can do about passports. I will ring the man in Spain and see what happens. I'm not promising anything lads, see what happens."

The four boys walk over to him tears in their eyes. Michael puts his hand on top of the caretaker's hand on the table. Jim puts his hand on Michael's. Tom and Dennis do the same. All looking at the caretaker they move away one by one knowing what is to come is a lot better than this hole.

Michael returned to the field shortly afterwards. He worked hard for three months, digging spuds, milking cows and general handy work. He met with the three boys once a week at the back of the church, no music just talk about the priests, some that left and a few new that had arrived. The caretaker did not associate with them much either. He knew since the concert that the cat was out of the bag but the priests never said a word to him. They got the organ and the Bishop was happy, they did not want to rock the boat. The Bishop's nephew had recorded the music and some of the money was going towards the orphanage. It was six months later that something happened. The lady and the caretaker were sitting in the kitchen. Michael had met him earlier in the field. He told him to meet him here at eight o'clock with the other boys. Michael and the three boys walked in silently. "Right lads, this is it." the caretaker says. "I have to move shortly. The white collar boys don't want me anymore, they have booked a place for me in Dublin but I won't go. I will go to Spain with you fellows. I rang my brother last month, everything is arranged." Looking at the woman, "She will help us. Mary will put you up in the basement in Galway. There are a few beds there and you will be alright but you cannot come out of the place, when you leave here the gardai will be looking for you. The first place they will look will be my place; I will be their prime suspect. I will be watched going to the airport and maybe in Spain, I don't know. On my own they can do nothing. I will have things organised when you arrive in Spain, do you understand? This should work lads," he says looking at the four boys, "if it doesn't we are all in the shit". He looks over at the lady and says in a rough voice "Organise passports as soon as possible. In Spain you cannot be sent back. That brother of mine did not come back for ten years and then they didn't want to know him. He was in Dublin; he came down here and cried outside the place. Even asked questions. The fact was he did not exist anymore."

Michael listened attentively to the story. Looking at his three buddies he thinks 'We will be alright; if we go down we will go down together.'

"I will try to hold my position here for as long as I can." the caretaker says. "For how long I don't know; now back to your rooms. I should have everything organised shortly. Good luck and no talk to anybody."

Michael returned to his room, to his bed. Lying down he goes into a cold sweat. 'If we are caught,' he thinks, 'God help us but, it is worth it and in Spain they will have more freedom and less trouble and maybe a better future and who knows we might be able to buy some good instruments at the right price.' Putting his hand under the pillow he puts his mother's medal into his hand. Closing his eyes he says "Give us some help, Mum." Drying his eyes he goes to sleep. His face changes from a frown to a smile as he dreams of freedom and music.

The caretaker got his orders two weeks later. They asked him to move to Dublin. He declared "I'm not leaving Galway. I will take whatever money is due to me and go."

One of the priests said to him "Where will you go?"

"None of your business." he replied. "Just give me my money and I will clear out."

A few days later a few of the priests came to him and said that he could stay. He knew himself that he had no proper cover in the place and no proper stamps. He told them he would not stay and that he had enough of the place.

When he left the orphanage nobody ever found out what the priests gave him.

He told Michael to meet him later in the kitchen. That night he cried in front of him saying "This is it lad, you will be leaving shortly your passports are ready. I will meet you at the back wall at 12 o'clock. There is a tunnel under it so you can move fairly fast. I will bring you in the van to Mary's place and you will stay in the cellar for four days, then two of you will go to Shannon and two of you will go to Dublin airport. I will meet you in the airport in Spain and there you will work for my brother. Poor wages but you will get your keep and tips at the restaurant. Your passports carry my name and my brother's wife will be your aunt. If the Spanish police ask any questions your mother died in Ireland and we moved here together. This should work. Ok Michael, if you want to back out now is the time." he says.

Michael stares into the man's eyes and says "How long will we be in Spain?"

"I don't know." the caretaker replies. "As soon as you get settled I will return. This is my home. You will have to stick it for at least five years. After that you can return here too without being caught by the law."

Michael shakes his hands saying "We are with you, I will tell the boys. I will see you at 12 o clock so Sunday night at the back of the wall beside the church."

After working in the fields that day Michael returned to the orphanage. He sees the three boys down the hall, a few priests beside them.

"What's wrong with you, young fellow?" one of the priests says to Michael. "You look frightened."

"I am," he replies, "by this place."

"Watch your mouth," the priest says, "and go and eat. We have mass at seven and one of you has to sing in the choir for Easter".

Michael goes into the kitchen and sits down. His three buddies come over to him. "Its Sunday night lads, 12 o clock, we go together. Out the window, down to the back of the church, okay?" he says staring at them.

"Okay." Jim replies.

"What about you Tom?"

"I'm in." he replies.

Dennis nods his head in agreement.

"Everything is arranged," Michael says, "Just play it cool until then. Bring a small amount of clothing and a few valuables that belong to your parents."

Michael packed his bag early Sunday morning. He put his mother's medal in his pocket after he kissed it. Frightened, he does not know what the outside world holds for him but he feels his buddies and himself should be alright. The caretaker and Mary say they would look after them. The priest asked them all to sing in the church Sunday evening four o'clock so they should all be together tonight. He will take the lock off the kitchen door and they should be ready to go at 11.30. After the Mass the four boys meet in the main room upstairs.

"We will have some grub lads and we will move at 11.30. If we take it easy and don't panic we will be alright. It's going to be rough for a few days but we will get through it alright lads."

Michael and the three boys stare at one another shaking and frightened but determined to succeed in their escape.

Chapter 14

That night, four shadows move ever so slowly towards the kitchen. The silence is disturbed by one of the priests banging on the main door. The boys keep very silent, afraid to move until the footsteps fade away in the hall. Opening the door, the four boys move across the kitchen towards the yard. Closing the backdoor, they move back towards the back of the church. Their shadows like ghosts in the moonlight. Going down on his knees, Michael moves the other three boys in front of him. The caretaker had his work well done. He had the bushes cut just beside the tunnel. As they move under the wall and come out the other side, Michael sees a light in front of him. 'A smart move' he thinks, 'its dark and the van won't be noticed and there is traffic coming and going on the main road.'

"You will have to jump in when the van is moving." a voice says. "I have changed my number plates; it's just if I stop someone will report the van when they discover you are missing." As the van moves along the highway slowly, the four boys move in the side door. The van moves out the main road. Nobody any the wiser what has happened. A passing driver looking at the van thinks it's somebody on a camping trip with English number plates who maybe got directions wrong. Nobody saw the four boys jump in, how could they, the van was moving. The lights were on and the van shielded them from the passing traffic.

The boys listened attentively to the caretaker as the van pulled into the house. Mary bangs the side of it and tells him to move around the back. The four jump out of the van down the stairs to the basement.

"This is your home for a few days; lads make the best of it. I will bring down tea and sandwiches shortly. Just sort yourselves out and try not to make too much noise the walls are fairly thin in this place."

Michael sits on the corner bed and smiles at his three buddies. Shaking with fright he says "We are doing alright lads we are half way there." The boys looked back at him, fear showing in their eyes but his words bring them hope for the world ahead. After the tea and sandwiches the boys moved to their bed. They are warm, each with a hot water bottle. That night, as Michael looks up at the ceiling, he smiles thinking 'Maybe we will make it after all. It's Monday. Two leave shortly and two leave Friday with a bit of luck we all meet in Spain on Saturday. What happens after God only knows but we won't be coming back here for a long time.'

.

The next morning the boys were up to the sound of moving traffic. They were beside a busy road with traffic moving in all directions. Michael stirs himself and puts his two feet on the ground. His three buddies stare at him from their beds. Tired and worried they look at one another. Michael is the first to speak. "Hungry?" he says looking over at Dennis.

He nods "Yes." not fully awake yet.

Michael stands up slowly moving his limbs towards the three boys. He says "We will get over this shit lads. This day week we will be together in a different country."

The three boys lift their heads slowly and look at him. Their faces show a slight tinge of excitement.

The lady comes down the stairs with the tray of brown bread and tea. "This will have to do until tonight." she says, sorting the delph out on the table. "The guards pulled the caretaker this morning up the road. They said they were looking for four boys that escaped from your place. Chances are they won't come here. Just read a few comics, I have your passports ready we will see tonight who goes first and who goes Friday. What happens when we get to Spain or what place we are going to I don't know." the lady said. "The man that owns the nightclub will meet us at the airport and he will look after you, you will have different names. He will be your uncle if anybody asks questions, your parents are dead and over there as long as you behave yourself you will be alright."

The four boys look at one another thinking, 'What does the future hold for them?'

Michael stands up in the middle and says "We all go or nobody goes. Nobody is backing down."

Dennis says, "Everybody including yourself is worried. We have been in a big orphanage for a long time. When we get to Spain we have to get education, learn the language it's not going to be easy."

The lady answers him back smartly "You have one thing going for you, you are orphans. The chances are, after a few years away, the authorities here will stop looking for you. When you were locked up in that big house nobody contacted you then and the chances are nobody ever will. The man you are going to owns a club 'The Witches Mountain' in Madrid. He will teach you Spanish and you will finish your education. He knows a few teachers over there. You will find it lonely, no English speaking friends. You will see English families together on holidays which will make you sad but you are all good lads and if you stay together and watch yourselves you will be coming back in five years or less."

The four boys glance at one another looking for answers. Michael speaks very slowly. "What do you think lads, will we see it through?"

The three boys stand on the floor. Jim is the first to speak saying "If we go down we go down together, okay lads?"

The lady climbed the stairs saying "Make up your minds who wants to go first or last."

"I will go tomorrow with Dennis" Jim says. "Michael, you and Tom can go Friday, if that is alright?"

"I don't mind." Michael says. Tom nods his head in agreement.

Jim and Dennis walk around wondering how to pass the time while Michael and Tom lie in the bed reading comics.

The lady opens the door and comes down the stairs. "Have you decided?" She asks.

"We have," Michael says Jim and Dennis go tomorrow with you."

"Alright." the lady replies. "I will bring down clothes after a while so you better have some rest. We will be leaving at 7 o clock to Shannon airport. I have your passports from the caretaker. He took your pictures one night when you were playing. Your names are different. Jim Doyle and Dennis Sweeney. I am your aunt. If anybody asks any questions show them your passports." Pointing to the other two boys she says "You will be getting your passports Thursday evening."

Michael goes over to the two boys and gives them a hug, tears forming in his eyes. "You are leaving shortly lads." Tom goes over and shakes their hands. Stone faced but a small tear from his eye showed that he will miss them. "I am not your boss or your leader," Michael says, "but we have been together a long time, we will be split up for a while but we will be together again in Spain. When we meet again on Sunday we will decide what we can do. If the jobs don't suit we will think of something else. Is that alright?" The four boys smile and hold hands. They know Michael is one of them, an orphan, a musician and a bloke that will stick with them through thick and thin to the bitter end.

Chapter 15

Jim and Dennis get dressed at sunrise. The lady comes down the stairs saying "It is 5.30."

"We know." the boys say, looking at the clock.

"Don't get nasty." the woman said. "I know it's hard on you but this day week you will be together in Madrid sitting around a table with ice cream and soft drinks, think of that." she smiles. "Say goodbye to your buddies, the fuzz are still looking for you, the sooner we get started the better."

"What about clothes?" Michael says sitting on the bed.

"I have them all in the van. Sorry lads, we have to move, say goodbye, I will wait upstairs".

They shake hands with one another. Jim shouts "Look after yourselves, we will see you shortly." The two boys climb up the stairs their heads down, sad, but determined to see the journey through. At the very top Jim and Dennis hold up their fingers making the sign for victory. The other two lads return the answer with the same sign.

The caretaker arrived that evening, a smile on his face saying "The boys arrived alright. You will see them on Friday". Michael does not smile neither does Tom. They miss their friends but they will meet them again in a few days. What the future holds they do not know or care as long as they stay together in the one place. They will be happy enough.

"I got a phone call from one of the priests yesterday, they are still looking for you but they will call off the hunt in a few days. The only friends and relatives you have are dead. One of you has a sister someplace but she cannot be traced. Don't look so down lads, I have your passports here we will go to Dublin Friday morning. We will be in Spain that evening at six o clock all being well. I'll get a bit of grub lads. Do you want to put on the small radio and listen to a bit of music?"

"No thanks," Michael says, "nothing is going to cheer us up until we meet the boys in Spain. We will play the music and listen to it as well."

The caretaker smiles down at Michael thinking he is right. They are four musicians, take one away and you have no musicians. "Alright lads," "he said, "the grub will be a bit rough for a while. Friday morning we will head for Dublin airport. Everything is ready. You have two different names, they are written on your passports. I am a bit nervous like yourselves. I don't know if I will come back at all."

"Why wouldn't you?" Michael says looking at him. "This is your town, you have friends. We have nobody and when we fly to Spain we will have nobody either."

"Don't worry," the caretaker replied, "you will be well looked after in Madrid. My brother has a restaurant and a nightclub. You will have to work hard for a while. He has your names. Any questions, he will vouch for you but you will have to knuckle down to work for a while."

Michael sits back on the bed and asks "What time Friday morning?"

The caretaker replies, "Five o'clock, the flight leaves at ten. You can go up top tonight and walk in the yard. With the other boys gone you should be alright. I will bring down the grub shortly."

That night, after they eat, the two boys climb up the stairs and up into the yard. It's dark and the only sound is from the passing traffic. Michael sits on the wall and looks across the dark horizon. Thinking, 'On beyond that mountain is a hell house where I was raised as a child'.

Looking at Tom beside him he says, "How do you feel buck?"

"I feel alright Michael, it's just I miss the boys a bit that is all."

"Sit down here a minute." Michael says. "Maybe if we sang a bit together it might brighten up the loneliness."

Michael takes the mouth organ out of his pocket. He smiles at Tom saying "What about a bit of blues?"

"You play, I will hum." Tom says.

Michael blows the mouth organ just with two notes. Tom claps his hands and sings a blues song he heard a few years ago. The silence of the night is broken to the sound of the two boys singing and playing. It brings a hopeful sound and a smile to the two boys.

Watching from the door, the caretaker, tears forming in his eyes. Talking to himself he says "I will miss you boys in the near future when I return home."

The two boys return to their beds that night, their heads down. Michael lies awake for a while thinking about his two buddies. After a while he looks over at his mate saying "Hey buck, are you alright?" Tom doesn't answer he just looks out at him from the bed and holds out his hand. Michael takes it and holds it tight "Goodnight old buddy," he says, "until tomorrow."

The next morning the two boys are woken by the caretaker. "The food is on the table lads, make the best of it, the next stop is Madrid. You will probably get something to eat on the plane."

Michael puts his belongings in the bag. The first thing he puts in is the medal his mother gave him and he is afraid he will lose it. "I am not hungry." he says to the caretaker.

"Me neither." Tom says.

The two climb up the stairs, heads down. They open the back of the van and climb in. "Check your passports lads, your names are inside with your picture. I am your uncle and you are going to see relatives there if anybody asks any questions. Alright lads, hold on it's a long trip to Dublin."

The two boys lie back in the van and go to sleep. They are awoken some time later as he parks the van outside the airport. "I will have to come back in a week just to sort things out but we will fly out together. Don't worry lads, you will be well looked after by my brother. He has been down the same road as yourselves."

Emptying the bags out of the van, they carry them towards the airport. At the main entrance Michael notices a priest. "What if this fellow recognises us?" he says.

The caretaker walks back and says, "He is not one of ours and, if he was, he wouldn't recognise how you boys are dressed."

At the counter, the check-in clerk looks at the two boys and says "Are you for a holiday lads?"

The caretaker answers, "Their father is in Spain, he is not well. He got a bit of a ticker problem last week. I am his brother; we are going to see him for a month. Chances are we will be all returned before that."

"Good luck to you," the girl replies, "I hope everything works out alright."

"It will," Michael replies smiling, "it will."

The boys board the plane, both thinking of the journey ahead. Tom looks at his buddy and says "How are you feeling?"

"Not great," Michael replies, "but, when the bird takes off, I will be alright."

As the plane ascends into the air, Michael looks through the glass. Seeing the sun shining through the clouds he looks down at the houses. He thinks about one big house. He hopes he will never again see the orphanage please God.

Chapter 16

When the plane hits the runway Michael awakes with the thump of the wheels. He had no seat belt on all the time. Rubbing his eyes he shakes a bit with fright. "What will this place hold for us Tom?" he says.

Tom does not reply, only beckons him to hurry up and move. "I hope the boys are here." he says.

"They will be," Michael replies, "they will be."

As the bus moves towards the airport, Michael glances towards the building wondering will they be here. As they move past security towards the main gate they see two boys with short trousers and tea shirts. Beside them is a lady with a large hat. "Look Tom," Michael says, "look over there, it is the two boys."

"Hold it." the caretaker says. "Don't get excited." But it's too late. When he looks again he sees four boys holding each other. What he does not see are the tears falling in front of them on the ground.

The four boys stick together for a few days. They stay in the night club upstairs. The caretaker organises different accommodation for them afterwards but they were never far away from one another. Their education was slow but they learned the Spanish very well from the local teacher. Michael worked in a paper shop for a while. Tom in a restaurant. Dennis got a job in the pub and Jim got a job as a cleaning boy in an apartment block. The caretaker returned to Galway shortly afterwards and they never saw him again. His only contact with them was a Christmas card. The music seemed to fall away for a while with the work and getting accommodation but it was one Sunday when the four boys walked along the beach that it hit them. They saw two boys playing guitars together. Watching them, Michael decided it was time for a change. "Come on boys, it is time to do a bit of shopping. We will have a look at the music shop at the back of the Palace Nightclub."

As he approaches the shop, Michael sees the owner at the door. "Are you open?" He asks.

"It doesn't matter," he replies, "you haven't any money to buy the stuff."

"We have a few pound," Michael says, "and if we don't buy it you can rent some of it out".

Moving inside the shop he asks his three buddies to look around the shop. Looking at the prices Michael bows his head and says "No way lads, no way." Drums, guitars out of line he thinks. "But maybe we could rent them." He says to Tom.

"Ask him." Dennis says.

As Michael goes towards the door he sees something on the counter that attracts his attention, a photograph of the caretaker and the man in the shop. "You know this fellow?" he asks.

"I do," the man replies, "he is my first cousin. He called here some time ago, said he brought a few orphans over from Galway."

Michael smiles up at the man thinking 'there is a resemblance, except for the pony tail'. "Have you his number?" he asks. "We are the boys he brought over."

The shop keeper smiles at the four boys saying "You are the musicians he talked about. Come over here and I will give him a ring."

As the man dials the number, the four lads look at the photograph and smile. The shopkeeper, the caretaker and the man at the club are standing in front of the shop. "Here, talk to him, the sound is not great but it is an improvement of what it used to be."

Michael talks to him for a minute and hands the phone to the other boys. As they finish talking he takes the phone back. Looking at the boys he smiles. "Alright," he says, "you can have the instruments on hire. You should have told me who you were". Watching them look around the shop he says "That caretaker friend of yours and me played music in Galway years ago. John is my name, here is my Card." giving it to Michael. "Follow me lads," he says, "I have some instruments out the back, we will sort something out." As he opens the sheds, the four boys see a set of drums and few old guitars. "I don't want to get smart with you boys but only that you turned up today, I was going to close the shed and sell it but, I am glad you came. Have a look and see what you think I will be outside if you want me."

The four boys look around the shed. They see photographs of Jimmy Hendricks, The Tremolos and Cat Stevens on the Walls. Michael remembers reading about them in the orphanage. Jim and Tom look at the guitars and Dennis looks at the drums. As they move towards the door they notice the man is closing the shop. "What money have you lads?" he asks.

"I don't know," Jim says, "the Spanish money is all shit but I have more money back in the flat."

"Throw it up on the table and we will count it." the man says. "You are not going too far with this lot." looking at the boys. "Tell you what," the man says, "there are three guitars and a set of drums plus amplifiers, I will rent them to you. The buck next door will give you a booking, I will see to that, but the money you make is mine for the first month".

Michael looks at him with a sour face and says "You are not doing us any favours. What happens after the month?"

"We will see." the owner says.

"We will see shit." Michael says. "Get us a booking for two months, the first month is yours, the next month is ours, instruments and all. We will see how the singing goes in the club and what happens." Michael says. "Make up the price of the instruments now, we will pay a deposit and we will come back Thursday after work and we will see what happens".

The following week the four boys got their job in the night club. The 'Witch House' it was called. Two nights a week they played rock music with another band. After two months they played five nights a week when their music proved very popular. The ladies will stand in front of them smiling and dancing and it was not long until they started dating. After two months the boys had their instruments paid for and they moved to different accommodation. It was one night in the club that Michael noticed something. Two men in the corner, one whose face looked familiar. Jim and Tom spied him as well. It was someone from the orphanage. He was a person who used to come and go fairly often. He was friendly with one of the priests, Tom Dempsey was his name. It was later that night that the four boys went to the table and said "Hello."

The man looks at the four boys saying "I don't know you."

"You did one time," Michael replies, "when you were in Galway. You were friendly with one of the priests there, Father Johnson."

"I knew him," the man replies, "so what?"

"He was one thick man." Jim says.

"What are you doing here?" Michael asks.

"I am here with my wife and son on holiday. You boys have a band; you are good I heard you tonight. My son might talk to you tomorrow about a recording contract. He is over here on business. He goes to all the clubs once a year looking for talent. Last year all he got was one band. Are you playing tomorrow night?" he asks.

"We are," Michael replies, "we start at 9 o' clock."

"Alright," the man says, "we will be here."

The man gets up from the table and walks away. Michael smiles thinking 'maybe it is a joke but we will see what will happen.'

The next evening the boys started playing. The man sat down at the table with two other younger men. The younger man stared at the boys all night. 'They were not too impressed with the music.' Michael thinks. When they finished up that night, he walks over to the band and asked them outside for a while.

Looking at the four boys he asks, "Which of you boys is the boss man?"

The three boys pointed Michael. "I don't know about that?" Michael says.

"Alright," he says, "I will give it to you straight. You are good. Not very good, but good. I know where you came from before you came here and I am not going to say anything. You cannot go back to that country for a while. Maybe they want you, maybe they don't. I own a recording studio. We will draw up an agreement next week. Everything will be legal. I won't rob you even though I could with the position you are in with the law. I will have a taxi outside here tomorrow morning. You will be brought to my villa, that is where the studio is. I will collect you at 12 o' clock. There will be refreshments served at the villa. If the recording works out, your records will be for sale in Spain, Germany and France. You will expand to other countries, maybe Ireland and England in a few years. Where the local position stands I don't know, the country can be funny too. I want two things from you before the week is out: The name of your band, you haven't got one, and two; some of you boys will have to start writing music or you won't survive. Until the morning Good night." the man says.

As the man walks away Michael thinks, 'You are a cocky boy aren't you but we will see what happens.' Michael says "Let's call it off until tomorrow. Jim and Tom leave the ladies at home. Dennis, you come with me and we will have a few drinks before the place closes."

Dennis smiles at Michael saying "It is funny".

"What's funny?" Michael replies.

"I get a strange feeling that fellow knows more about us than what he is saying."

"Why do you think that?" Michael says.

"I don't know that," Dennis replies putting the drink to his mouth, "but I have a strange feeling that fellow was brought up in an orphanage."

It was only in later years Dennis was proved right. He came over here with his adoptive parents and never went back. His adoptive parents were musicians. Even though he didn't play, he started a studio in Spain and had been very successful. The boys met at the studio the next day. They recorded some of the Beatles songs and a few others. It was the beginning of their career.

Two months after the recording, Michael and the boys were back in their own villa. Looking around, Michael smiles, "I suppose it was worth it all to get this far."

Jim and Dennis are behind him sitting down. The two ladies at the pool, enjoying the evening shade. Michael thinks there are marriages brewing there. Tom sits over in the corner strumming his guitar. He has written some good songs lately, they will be on the new recording. Jim and Tom hum a small bit to the sound of the guitar. Turning his head around, Michael stares around into the blue ocean and thinks to himself, 'Just beyond the setting sun is Ireland and in that small island is an orphanage, a place I don't want to see again.' But they will return to the city some day to play and maybe see some of their old buddies from the place, but the man they will be looking for is somebody with a ring on his ear and a pony tail and maybe a shovel and a brush, their caretaker friend. 'Funny,' Michael thinks, 'he never told us his full name but his face shines out in the ocean and the music behind him shows a sign of hope and joy in the years ahead.'

Conclusion

Michael stares at the building from his sitting position. He thinks about the lads in the band. They had some good times after that. Jim and Dennis got married but it didn't last. Too much time away from home. They got divorced shortly afterwards. Still good friends, both had kids who they treated very well, often brought them to concerts in London and France. Tom wrote some good music. Never married, just turned a bit weird with drugs and drink. There was a lot of trouble after they left Spain, touring around Europe. A lot of fights off stage but Michael seemed to hold it together both on and off the stage. When they played they were the best. Two years ago they were going to split up but the new name made them close again. They named the band 'The Wild Boys', it suited them a lot better.

Michael stirs himself from his seat and takes one last look at the cold building. Evening is coming slowly and a dark cloud hovers over the building, giving it a ghostly look.

Pulling his coat around him, he moves down towards the gate. He sees a blackbird and a pigeon in the trees. Smiling, he thinks 'I have nothing to give you only this,' picking the money out of his pocket. Putting it back, he opens the rusty gate and sees something which gives him a start.

The three boys standing along the wall. "We knew you would come" Dennis said, pushing his long hair back.

"We knew in the past that sometime you would want to see this old place. You do a lot of talking in your sleep," Jim says, "especially with drink."

Dennis hands him a naggen of brandy, "Take a slug," he says, "the concert doesn't start for four hours and it will help you forget about this place."

"No," Michael replies, "that stuff and me will have to part company. I am going for treatment shortly lads, the bottle has taken over a bit."

The boys smile at him, it is not the first time he has said that, even though his voice seems more determined. The four boys put their hands around one another and march towards the hotel, getting ready for the concert. They don't notice the two men standing outside the funeral parlour, 'McMillan & Son', Funeral Directors.

"I think it is over for today son." one of them says.

"It is," the young man replies, "the burial is at 12 o'clock tomorrow."

As the young lad locks the door, he scratches his face and says "It's strange it is, very strange."

"What is strange?" the old man says.

"Well, he worked in that place across the road as a caretaker one time."

"What is strange about that lad?" the man says.

"Nothing," he replies, "it is just that before he died, he gave one of the nurses something to put in the coffin which was to be buried with him."

"Get to the point lad; it is getting cold out here."

"Well, I did put it in right now and I won't take it out for anybody. It was a news cutting from the 'Galway Chronicle'."

"The paper must be worth something." the old man says.

"It was worth nothing," the young lad shouts at him, "it contained some news about a rock band and a photograph of four boys and the heading read 'The boys are back in town.'

End

This book is dedicated to all musicians living and dead.

Music. Sometimes you play because you have
to play. Sometimes you play because you
want to play and sometimes you play.

18101ZUK00001B/11/P

Lightning Source UK Ltd.
Milton Keynes UK
UKOW05225026101 1